Not in the House, Newton!

By Judith Heide Gilliland

Illustrated by Elizabeth Sayles

CLARION BOOKS/*New York*

Clarion Books
a Houghton Mifflin Company imprint
215 Park Avenue South, New York, NY 10003
Text copyright © 1995 by Judith Heide Gilliland
Illustrations copyright © 1995 by Elizabeth Sayles

The illustrations for this book were executed in pastel.
The text is set in 16/20-point Cochin.

Printed in the USA

Library of Congress Cataloging-in-Publication Data

Gilliland, Judith Heide.
Not in the house, Newton! / Judith Heide Gilliland ; illustrated by Elizabeth Sayles.
p. cm.
Summary: Everything Newton draws with his magic red crayon becomes real, and
heeding his mother's admonition he flies the airplane he draws right out the window.
ISBN 0-395-61195-4
[1. Drawing—Fiction. 2. Crayons—Fiction. 3. Magic—Fiction.] I. Sayles, Elizabeth, ill. II. Title.
PZ7.G4155No 1995
[E]—dc20 94-11792
CIP
AC

HOR 10 9 8 7 6 5 4 3 2 1

For Roxy: my twin, my hero
—*J. H. G.*

To Daniel and Jessica
—*E. S.*

When Newton found a red crayon lying in the grass next to the sidewalk in front of his house, he knew at once it was magic.

It was extraordinarily red. Not light red or orange red or dark red or blue red, but RED red.

He put it in his pocket. It felt warm.

Newton went into his house and asked his mother for a piece of paper.

"Here, dear," said Newton's mother. "You may have a whole box."

The paper was very white.

"And here are your crayons, Newton," said Newton's mother. "I'm glad you are going to do something nice and quiet like drawing. I am going to be busy getting ready for our guests tonight."

Newton carried the paper to his room. By now he could feel the crayon humming quietly in his pocket.

He examined the red crayon. It was even redder than before, and shiny.

Carefully, Newton started to draw a ball. It was going to be a red ball, of course, very round and very beautiful.

Newton loved drawing.

Just as he colored in the very last bit of red, the ball bounced off the page.

Newton caught it. For a while he bounced it off the wall. To his surprise, he caught it each time.

"Where did you get that ball, Newton?" asked Newton's mother. She was standing in the doorway with the vacuum cleaner hose.

"I drew it," said Newton.

"What a good artist you are! But you know the rule about balls. Not in the house, Newton." She went back to her vacuuming.

Newton put the ball in his sweatshirt pocket. He took another piece of paper and, after thinking about it for a minute or two, began to draw a red racecar.

Newton could tell this was going to be his best racecar ever.

Just as he finished putting in the headlights, the car rolled off the page and into his hand.

Newton liked the feel of it. He set it on the floor and gently vrroomed it across the carpet.

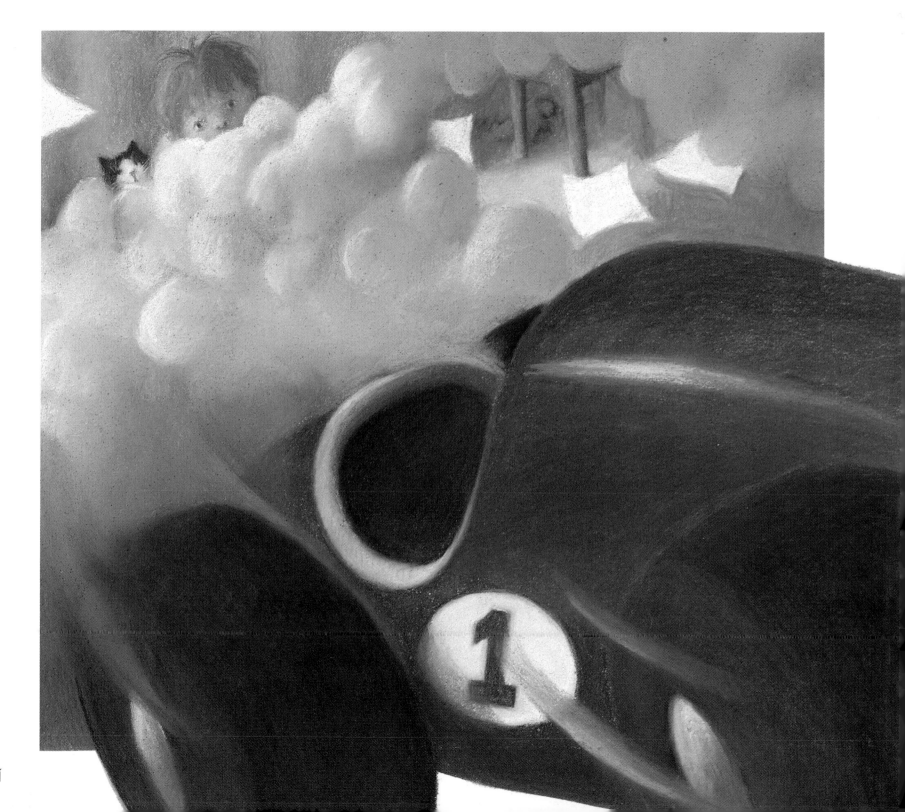

It took off like a jet across the floor, up the wall, across the ceiling, down the opposite wall, and back to Newton. It stopped in front of him with a squeal of brakes.

"Where did you get that car?" asked Newton's mother. She was standing in the doorway with a folded tablecloth.

"I drew it," said Newton.

"Think of that!" she said, turning away. "But remember, racecars belong outside, not in the house, Newton."

WIHHHH
WIHHHH
WIHHHH
WIHHHHA

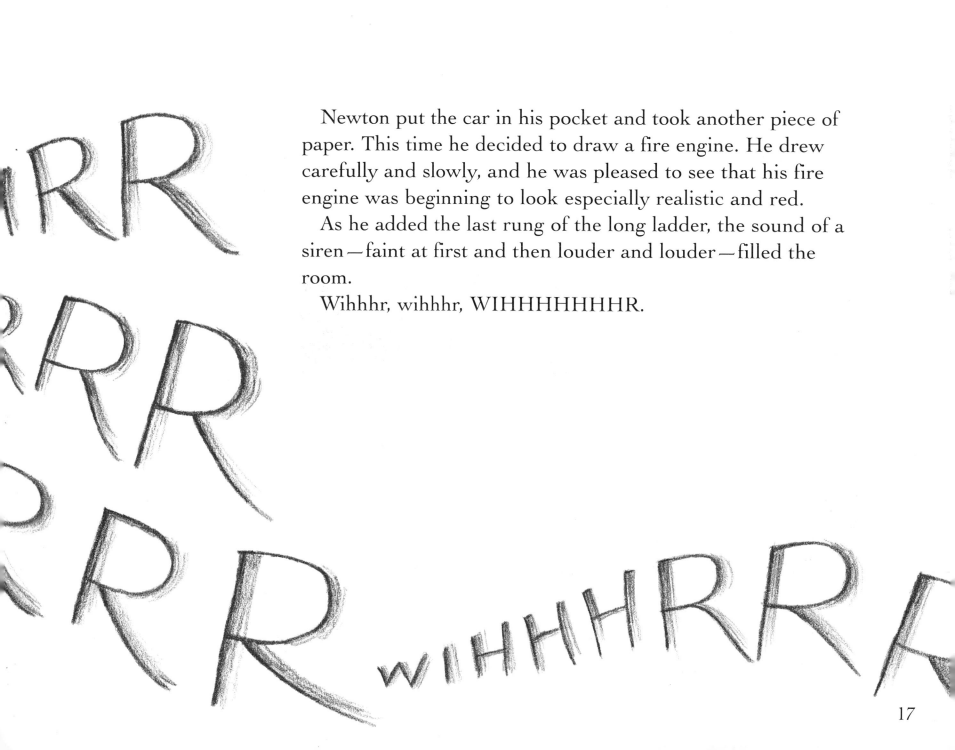

Newton put the car in his pocket and took another piece of paper. This time he decided to draw a fire engine. He drew carefully and slowly, and he was pleased to see that his fire engine was beginning to look especially realistic and red.

As he added the last rung of the long ladder, the sound of a siren—faint at first and then louder and louder—filled the room.

Wihhhr, wihhhr, WIHHHHHHHR.

"Where did you get that fire engine?" asked Newton's mother. She was standing in the doorway with the candlesticks.

"I drew it," said Newton.

"Your Uncle Gus is a fine artist too. Maybe it runs in the family," said Newton's mother. "But you know you shouldn't make loud noises, not in the house, Newton."

Newton got another piece of paper.

He was hungry, so he drew a few red apples. They looked good enough to eat, so he ate them. They were unusually crisp and cool and crunchy.

What should he draw next? He thought about boots. Boots are nice, especially when they are red.

And *red* red boots might be even nicer.

Newton drew red boots. First the feet, then the tops. He was thinking about adding a zipper or a buckle or something when the boots jumped off the page and onto the floor.

Newton put them on. They fit perfectly. They felt and looked so much like special boots that Newton wondered if they might not be special jumping boots. He took a small jump and just missed bumping his head on the ceiling.

"No jumping in the house, Newton," said Newton's mother as she passed his doorway.

Newton stopped jumping.

He looked at his stack of white paper. There were still many sheets left. He looked at his magic red crayon. It was as red and as magical looking as ever.

"Can I have some tape?" he asked his mother.

"What a good idea, Newton. I'm glad you want to do a nice quiet project. I'll give you a whole roll." Newton's mother brought him a big roll of tape from her desk.

After she left the room, Newton painstakingly laid out the rest of the sheets of paper on the floor, making sure the edges were even and only just touching one another. He pulled out long strips of tape. He was careful not to let the tape get twisted and stuck to itself. Slowly he taped the sheets together. It was a hard project and it took a long time, but when he had finished he had a giant piece of paper on the floor.

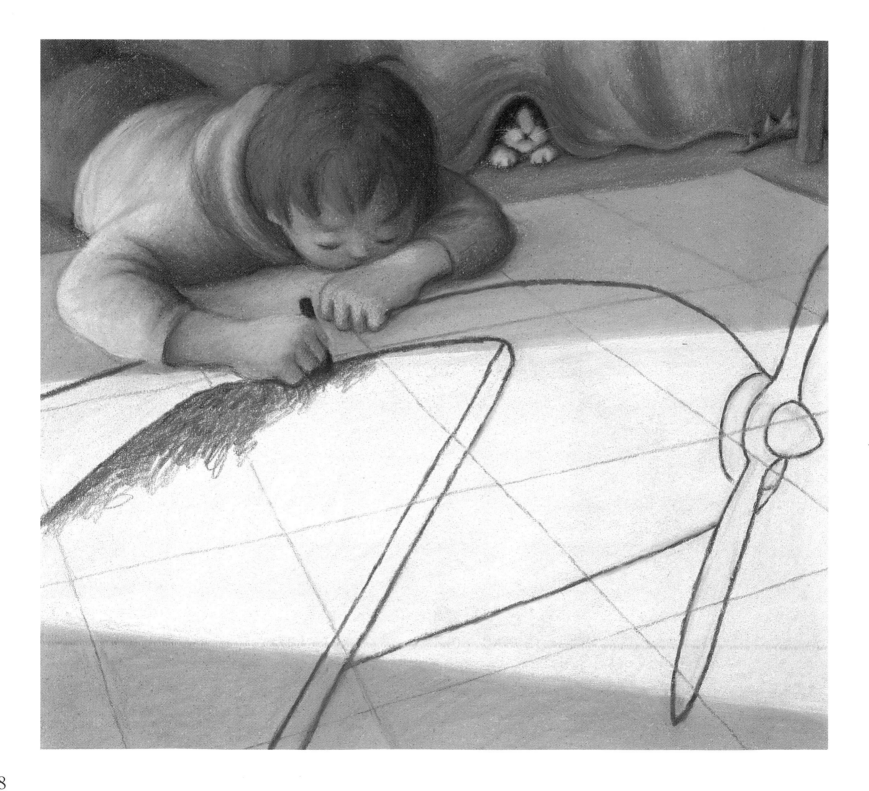

"Now comes the hard part," thought Newton. Making himself as light as possible, he lay on the paper and began to draw.

He drew and drew, taking care to make the wings perfectly balanced and the propeller large enough.

He could see this was going to be the best airplane he had ever drawn.

As he finished coloring in the door handle, the door of the airplane opened. Newton climbed in. The key was already in the ignition.

Newton turned the key. The engine roared and the propeller spun faster and faster until it was just a blur. He pulled the stick gently and the plane rose from the floor.

He was flying.

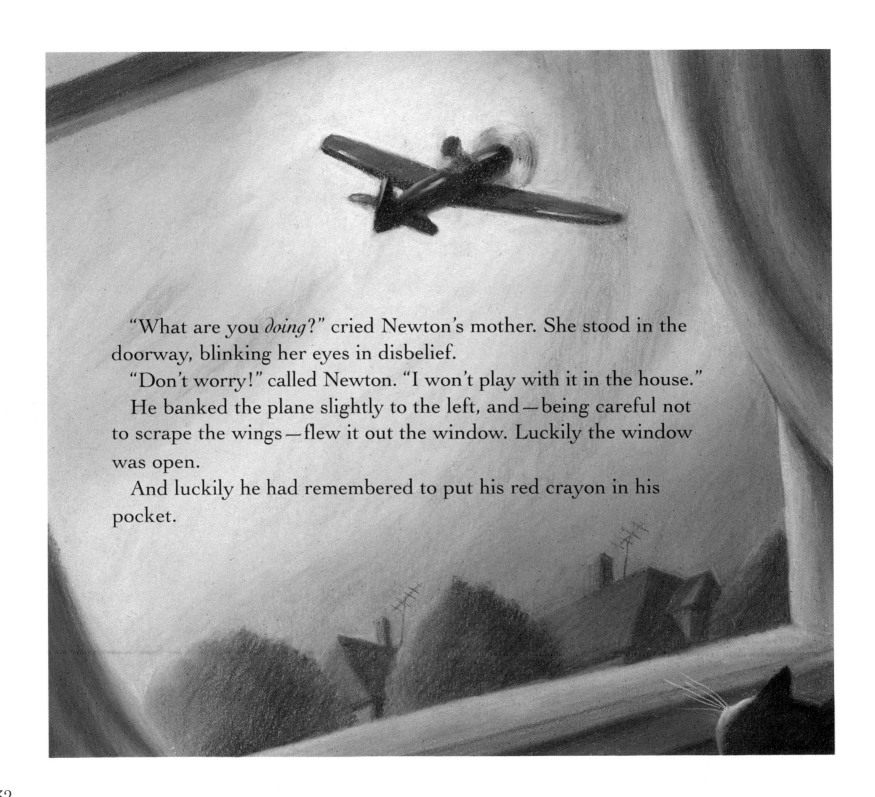

"What are you *doing*?" cried Newton's mother. She stood in the doorway, blinking her eyes in disbelief.

"Don't worry!" called Newton. "I won't play with it in the house."

He banked the plane slightly to the left, and—being careful not to scrape the wings—flew it out the window. Luckily the window was open.

And luckily he had remembered to put his red crayon in his pocket.